The Night Before Christmas

CLEMENT C. MOORE

ILLUSTRATED BY KATE JASPERS

Longmeadow Press

Twas the night before Christmas
when all through the house
Not a creature was stirring,
not even a mouse;
The stockings were hung
by the chimney with care,
In hopes that St Nicholas
soon would be there;

The children were nestled
all snug in their beds,
While visions of sugar-plums
danced in their heads;

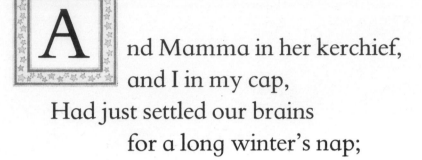

And Mamma in her kerchief,
and I in my cap,
Had just settled our brains
for a long winter's nap;

10

When out on the lawn
there arose such a clatter,
I sprang from the bed
to see what was the matter.

way to the window
    I flew like a flash,
Tore open the shutters
        and threw up the sash.
The moon, on the breast
        of the new-fallen snow,
Gave the lustre of midday
        to objects below,
When, what to my wondering eyes
        should appear,
But a miniature sleigh,
        and eight tiny reindeer,

13

With a little old driver,
    so lively and quick,
I knew in a moment
    it must be St Nick.
More rapid than eagles
    his coursers they came,
And he whistled, and shouted,
    and called them by name;

'Now, Dasher! now, Dancer!
  now, Prancer and Vixen!
On, Comet! on, Cupid!
  on, Donner and Blitzen!
To the top of the porch!
  to the top of the wall!
Now dash away! dash away!
  dash away all!'

15

As dry leaves that before
    the wild hurricane fly,
When they meet with an obstacle,
    mount to the sky;
So up to the house-top
    the coursers they flew,
With the sleigh full of Toys,
    and St Nicholas too.
And then, in a twinkling,
    I heard on the roof
The prancing and pawing
    of each little hoof.

As I drew in my head,
　　　and was turning around,
Down the chimney St Nicholas
　　　came with a bound.
He was dressed all in fur,
　　　from his head to his foot,
And his clothes were all tarnished
　　　with ashes and soot;
A bundle of Toys
　　　he had flung on his back,
And he looked like a pedlar
　　　just opening his pack.

19

is eyes – how they twinkled!
his dimples how merry!
His cheeks were like roses,
       his nose like a cherry!
His droll little mouth
       was drawn up like a bow,
And the beard of his chin
       was as white as the snow;
The stump of a pipe
       he held tight in his teeth,
And the smoke it encircled
       his head like a wreath;

He had a broad face
		and a little round belly
That shook, when he laughed,
		like a bowlful of jelly.
He was chubby and plump,
		a right jolly old elf,
And I laughed, when I saw him,
		in spite of myself;
A wink of his eye
		and a twist of his head,
Soon gave me to know
		I had nothing to dread;

23

He spoke not a word,
　　but went straight to his work,
And he filled all the stockings;
　　then turned with a jerk,
And laying his finger
　　aside of his nose,
And giving a nod,
　　up the chimney he rose;

24

H e sprang to his sleigh,
to his team gave a whistle,
And away they all flew
like the down of a thistle.

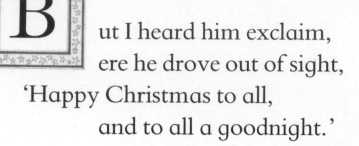

ut I heard him exclaim,
    ere he drove out of sight,
'Happy Christmas to all,
    and to all a goodnight.'

This edition published by Longmeadow Press
201 High Ridge Road
Stamford, CT 06904

This edition Copyright © 1987 Octopus Books Limited

ISBN 0–681–40255–5

Printed in the United Kingdom